Me
by me.

Me
by me.

The Pets.com Sock Puppet Book.

ibooks

Ben Asen is the photographer

Special Thanks to:

Karen Gould, Melissa Menta and Amy Robinson at Pets.com; Scott Duchon, Paul Schmidt, Lew Willig and Rob Smiley at TBWA/Chiat/Day San Francisco; The Back Fence in Greenwich Village, NY; Café Rock in Cranford, NJ; The Crossroads in Garwood, NJ; Eastman News in Cranford, NJ; Sound Station in Westfield, NJ and Jeanine Campbell.

Pets.com is an online retailer of pet products, information, and resources. Offering a broad product selection and expert advice from a staff of pet-industry experts and veterinarians, Pets.com gives consumers the confidence that they are providing their pets with the best possible care.

ibooks, inc.
24 West 24th Street
New York, NY10010

The ibooks World Wide Web Site address is:
http://www.ibooksinc.com

You can visit the ibooks Web site for a free read and download the first chapters of all the ibooks titles: http://www.ibooksinc.com

ISBN 0-7434-1313-X
First Pocket Books printing December 2000
10 9 8 7 6 5 4 3 2 1

Edited by Dinah Dunn
Cover photography by Ben Asen
Cover and interior design by Mike Rivilis

Printed in the U.S.A

Foreward

"Me by Me" is a labor of love for me.
While most books ~~had~~ take a couple of years
to come together. This one only took me
a couple of hours. But in dog years a
couple of hours is like a couple of human
years.. I think? Well, I could be wrong.
But the point is, it's not easy to turn a
roll of film into a book. And it's even
harder when you don't have opposable thumbs.

You know a lot of critics have said it
can't be done, puppets don't know how
to make books. And to ~~those~~ critics I
say... you're right. I had no idea what
I was doing. So if there are any mistakes
or inconsistencies be thankful I only tried
to make a book. Imagine what the problems
would be if I tried to make a bridge
or a dam.

When this guy took
the first shot right
into the sun, I
knew I was in
trouble. →

You know how some
people have that
~~you~~ insomnia problem
where ~~they~~ can't sleep?
Well, I don't have
that problem.

Recipe for Parakeet Pasta
- 4 pounds of spaghetti
- 2 jars of tomato sauce
- 1 jar of garlic
- ~~3~~ no parakeets

* Uncle Wiggles is my best friend and a parakeet. And I would never hurt him... on purpose.

Songs I know by heart. Sorta.

Karaoke is an art form. You have to play with the audience. Let's say I'm doing the original "Candle in the Wind" song and then I throw in some of the lyrics from the "Diana" version to catch them off guard. That's when the tears start pouring down. It's a gift.

You do not want to
test my knowledge
of music. Believe me,
I am like a sponge
when it comes to gr
groups and song
titles. Except for the
stuff before 1972 and
after 1982.

*"Signs, signs every-
where are signs."*

Friends

So this is where my pen pals live. No wonder they haven't R.S.V.P.'d to any of my pool parties.

This is the Interactive Part

1. Below is a list of my friends.
2. Match the friends on the list to the friends in the pictures.
3. With a line. The lines should start at the name and go to the picture that you think goes with the name the line is coming from.
4. Use a pencil so you can erase if you make a mistake.

5. ✱ You may notice that I'm in some of the pictures. But my name isn't on the list. So don't worry about trying to connect me with a line to any of the pictures of my friends.

Lulu
Whitey
miss Binkles
Cornwallis
Tigris and Euphrates
Leonardo

Brandon
Willard and Two Bits
Uncle Wiggles

My favorite
people.

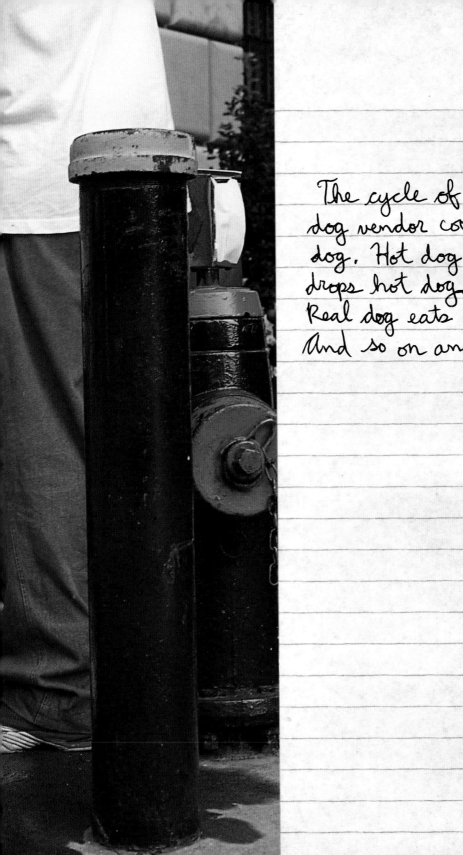

The cycle of life. Hot dog vendor cooks hot dog. Hot dog vendor drops hot dog on ground. Real dog eats hot dog. And so on and so forth.

I have three words
for you. Check.
Mate.

Arm Wrestling Career

Wins	losses
~~8~~	~~102~~
152	0

I love this guy because no matter how many times I beat him, he always comes back for more. He's got a lot of heart. But very poor technique.

For dogs, it's all about the thrill of the hunt. Stalking that piece of roast beef until it finally gives in. Victory!

The thrill of my life was meeting Chachi. But it turned really weird cuz I said "Chachi you are one of my heroes." Then he said, "my name is Scott." Then I said "you're crazy, you're Chachi." He said "that was my character's name." Then I said "thanks for shattering my world, Scott."

My favorite places.

I've failed quite a
few driving tests so
I've become all too
familiar with the
D.M.V. They set
you up to fail.
These signs were not
here last time.

This is how I meet females. I sit at a high traffic café table. I pretend to read some interesting literature and I $ also pretend to talk to my friend Uncle Wiggles. But really, it's all an act. Don't tell anyone.

9th street and 3rd. Avenue
My pilgrimage is complete.

Thoughts on life

Seeing beauty in the smallest things brings me the greatest joy.
The ocean breeze.
The little hermit crabs burrowing in the sand.
The sun glistening off the still blue water.
Ow! The hermit crabs!

Spending ~~sm~~ time alone to reflect on my life is usually pretty boring. So then I pick up a rock and try skipping it. Sometimes I'll get two skips. Sometimes three. And if I get a really good rock, I might get four. That's pretty much the best part of spending time alone, reflecting

At first I thought these were big sailboats that were far away. Then I realized they were small sail boats that were close to me. Weird.

Heroes

I know it looks like I saw a lot of good shows, but I really didn't. You see, I waited outside the venues for the show to end and picked up the ticket stubs that people threw ~~out~~ away. As far as the pictures go (of the musicians), Wiggles wrote away for them. Wiggles really knows how to stroke a rock star's ego, so of course they sent him back their pictures.

(This page)
I am amazed with birds. I don't know how they do it. They just flap their tiny little arms and fly all over the place. They build houses in trees. They make funny noises. I wish I could be a bird for a day.

(Other Page)
He's Eric Estrada, And the rest of us just wish we were.

Ahh... the elixer of life. A special
concoction that has just the right bite
and happens to be the perfect
refreshment for any occasion.

I've tried holding my breath before. And
the best I could do was like 24 seconds. →
These guys do it for their whole lives.

What happened on that field is classified. But I heard he saved 45 G.I.'s before he fetched the wrong grenade.

I wasn't gonna cry.